OTHER YEARLING BOOKS YOU WILL ENJOY:

SOMETHING QUEER AT THE BALL PARK, *Elizabeth Levy*

SOMETHING QUEER AT THE HAUNTED SCHOOL, *Elizabeth Levy*

SOMETHING QUEER AT THE LEMONADE STAND, *Elizabeth Levy*

SOMETHING QUEER AT THE LIBRARY, *Elizabeth Levy*

SOMETHING QUEER IS GOING ON, *Elizabeth Levy*

LIZZIE LIES A LOT, *Elizabeth Levy*

CHOCOLATE FEVER, *Robert Kimmel Smith*

UPCHUCK SUMMER, *Joel L. Schwartz*

THE TERRIBLE TRUTH, *Stephen Roos*

MY HORRIBLE SECRET, *Stephen Roos*

YEARLING BOOKS/YOUNG YEARLINGS/YEARLING CLASSICS are designed especially to entertain and enlighten young people. Patricia Reilly Giff, consultant to this series, received her bachelor's degree from Marymount College and a master's degree in history from St. John's University. She holds a Professional Diploma in Reading and a Doctorate of Humane Letters from Hofstra University. She was a teacher and reading consultant for many years, and is the author of numerous books for young readers.

For a complete listing of all Yearling titles, write to
Dell Readers Service,
P.O. Box 1045,
South Holland, IL 60473.

Something Queer on Vacation

(a mystery)

by
Elizabeth Levy
illustrated by
Mordicai Gerstein

A Yearling Book

Published by
Dell Publishing
a division of
Bantam Doubleday Dell Publishing Group, Inc.
666 Fifth Avenue
New York, New York 10103

To Fire Island

ISBN: 0-440-47968-1

Reprinted by arrangement with Delacorte Press
Printed in the United States of America

July 1982

20   19   18   17   16   15   14   13   12   11

CWO

"This week we're going to win," said Gwen as she and Jill ran down to the beach. Every Sunday there was a sandcastle contest. Gwen and Jill had built a lot of castles, but they had never won.

"I'll help you," said Gwen's little sister Nan.

"No," said Gwen. "You're too messy."

Fletcher started to dig a hole in the sand to keep cool.

"Why don't you help Fletcher dig a hole?" suggested Gwen.

"I don't want to," said Nan, and she wandered off down the beach.

"HOW TO MAKE DRIP TOWERS"

MIX EQUAL PARTS OF SAND AND WATER AND TAKE A BIG HANDFUL.

THEN, MAKE A FIST AND LET THE SAND DRIBBLE OUT THE BOTTOM.

WITH A LITTLE PRACTICE, THE DRIBBLES PILE UP AND MAKE TOWERS.

Gwen and Jill worked on their sandcastle all morning. For once their drip towers soared rather than drooped.

"I'm hungry," said Jill. "Let's go eat."

"What about Fletcher?" asked Gwen. Fletcher was asleep in his hole.

"Let him sleep," said Jill. "He's tired."

"He's always tired," said Gwen.

When Gwen and Jill came back after
lunch, Fletcher was lying smack on top of
their castle. He had squashed it. Only one
tower remained.

"Oh, no!" cried Gwen. "You bad dog!"

Jill dragged Fletcher off the squashed castle.

Gwen stared at the ruins. She bent down and picked up a crust of bread that had been under Fletcher. A tiny piece of salami clung to the crust.

(A CLOSE - UP OF THE TINY PIECE OF SALAMI)

(RYE BREAD)

"Salami," said Gwen, tapping her braces. She always tapped her braces whenever something queer was going on.

"You can't be hungry," said Jill. "We just had lunch."

"No, I mean that Fletcher loves salami," Gwen explained. "It's the only thing that could make him move. Someone put salami on our castle so he'd ruin it."

"Do you think someone wanted to win so badly that they cheated?" asked Jill.

Gwen nodded her head. "Come on. I bet it was someone nearby."

TAP
TAP
TAP
TAP
TAP
TAP TAP
TAP
TAP TAP
TAPPY
TAP
TAP
TAP TAP
TAPPITY
TAP
TIP-TAP
TAP

TAP TAP
TAP
TAP TAP
TAP
TAP TAP
TAP
TAP TAP
TAP
TAP TAP
TAP
TAP

George was the closest. His castle was square and neat.

"What did you have for lunch today?" asked Gwen.

"Peanut butter and mayonnaise," said George. "Why?"

"Never mind," said Gwen.

Gwen and Jill walked down the beach, questioning everyone.

Philip said he had liverwurst for lunch.

"I didn't have time for lunch," said Joanne. "I was too busy finishing my moat."

Nobody on the beach admitted eating a salami sandwich.

Gwen and Jill watched as the judges awarded First Prize to Joanne.

"Too bad your dog squashed your castle," said Joanne as she walked by. She looked very happy.

"Maybe it *was* just an accident," said Jill sadly.

"Or maybe that's what Joanne *wants* us to think," said Gwen.

The next Sunday was the last contest before the big July Fourth final. Gwen and Jill worked slowly and carefully until their castle was nearly perfect. It had crisscrossing tunnels and eight drip towers. They took Fletcher with them when they went up to the house for lunch.

When they came back to the beach, they couldn't believe their eyes.

Their castle was wrecked! Again! All the towers had been pushed down and the tunnels bashed in. Jill sat down next to the ruins and started to cry. Fletcher tried to lick her tears away.

"This time nobody can say it was an accident," Gwen said angrily. She examined the ruins. Strange webbed footprints led away from their castle to the ocean.

"That's who wrecked our castle," said Gwen, pointing to the footprints.

"A sea monster?" whispered Jill.

"No," said Gwen. "Those are flipper tracks. The person who smashed our castle was wearing rubber flippers."

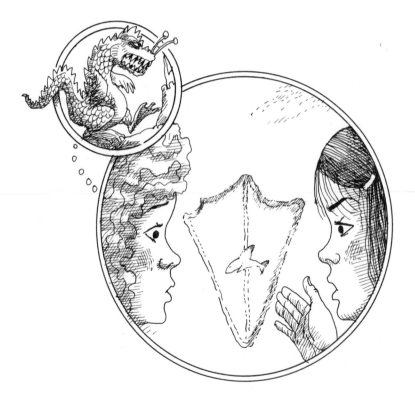

LARGE DEEP FLIPPER PRINTS MADE BY A LARGE HEAVY ANIMAL.

Gwen tapped her braces. "These flipper prints aren't very big," she said. "And they aren't very deep. In school we learned that you can tell how heavy an animal is by how deep its footprints are."

SMALL SHALLOW FLIPPER PRINTS MADE BY A SMALL SKINNY ANIMAL.

Gwen circled the ruins, tapping her braces.

Fletcher followed her.

"I got it!" cried Gwen. "It was a skinny...salami-eating... flipper-footed fink!"

"Philip's skinny," said Jill thoughtfully. "But so's Joanne, and so is George. Lots of kids on this beach are skinny."

A SKINNY, SALAMI-EATING, FLIPPER-FOOTED FINK!

Gwen stopped and peered at the web-
print. She pointed to a trademark design in
the middle.

"It looks like a shark," said Gwen. "And
there's a piece missing from one of the toes.
If we find the flippers that match these
prints, we can tell the judges."

Nearby, George was making a round castle with seaweed flags.

Gwen and Jill ran over. "Did you use flippers to get that seaweed?" asked Gwen.

"No," said George, "I don't own flippers."

"George could be lying," said Gwen as they walked away. "He says he doesn't own flippers, but he could be hiding them."

"I don't think George is a liar," said Jill. They stopped at Joanne's castle.

"Are those your flippers?" asked Gwen, and she tapped her braces.

"Yes," said Joanne. "Why are you tapping your braces?"

Casually Jill turned over Joanne's flippers.

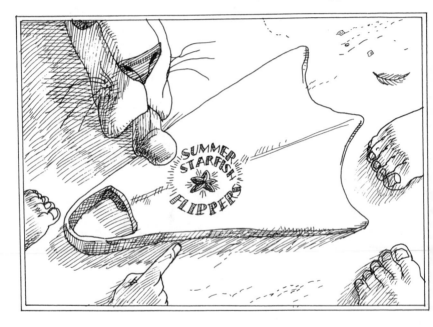

They had a starfish trademark underneath.
Jill shook her head. "No shark. Come on,
Gwen," she said. Joanne looked puzzled.
Gwen and Jill walked away.

Next they found Philip, who was building an octagon castle.

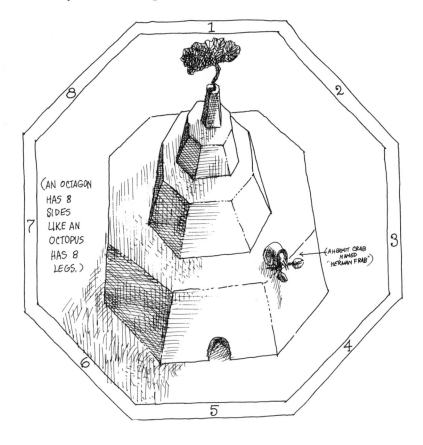

1

2

3

4

5

6

7

8

(AN OCTAGON HAS 8 SIDES LIKE AN OCTOPUS HAS 8 LEGS.)

(A HERMIT CRAB NAMED "HERMAN FRAB")

"Where are your flippers, Philip?" asked Gwen.

"Have you flipped?" said Philip. "I don't have any flippers."

Gwen and Jill checked every flipper
they could find. None matched.

George's round castle with the seaweed flags won that week's contest.

"We never win," said Jill sadly. "We never even have a chance."

Gwen shook her fist. "We're going to build the best castle for the July Fourth contest, and we're going to make *sure* it doesn't get wrecked."

All week Gwen and Jill
studied drawings of castles.
They collected shells to put on
the ramparts and beach glass to
use as windows.

"Have you come up with a plan to catch the person who keeps wrecking our castles?" asked Jill.

"No," admitted Gwen. "I still don't even know who it is."

"You'd better think fast," said Jill. "We don't have much time."

On July Fourth Gwen and Jill got up at sunrise. So did George, Philip, Joanne, and many other people who wanted to enter.

The prizes for the July Fourth contest were a trophy in the shape of a sandcastle and a dragon kite to fly on the beach.

As they worked the sun got very hot. Gwen and Jill were halfway finished when Fletcher started to dig a hole to keep cool.

"I'm hot too," said Jill. "I need a swim. Let's take turns so one of us can guard our castle."

"Suppose we both hid in the water," said Gwen thoughtfully. "With our masks and our snorkels we can stay close by and spy. The castle-wrecker will think our castle is unguarded."

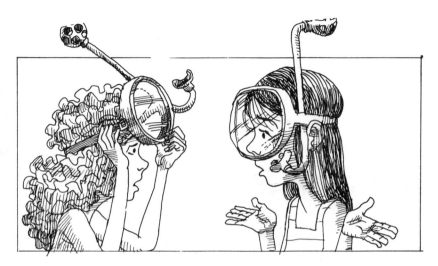

"But they could wreck it before we got out," objected Jill.

"We can be out in time," said Gwen. "We'll be able to see them, but they won't see us."

Gwen and Jill put on their flippers, masks,
and snorkels. They floated just a little way off
shore.

After a while they saw someone wearing
flippers and a mask approaching their castle.
Fletcher stood up and wagged his tail.

Gwen and Jill raced out of the water. The castle-wrecker took off down the beach, running awkwardly because of the flippers.

Gwen and Jill took off their flippers and flew down the beach after the masked and flippered person. Fletcher followed.

Fletcher took a flying leap and grabbed a flipper. The castle-wrecker fell in the sand.

Gwen and Jill ran to see who it was.
It was Nan!
Fletcher was licking her fingers.
"You're the salami-eating fink!"
shouted Gwen. "My own sister."

Nan blushed a deep red. "It was just an accident...
at least the first time," she stammered. "I was so mad
because you wouldn't let me help that I dumped my
sandwich on your castle to make it look messy."

"I bet you ate salami again today," said Gwen, tapping her braces.

"How did you know that?" asked Nan.

"Because Fletcher chased you," said Gwen. "He thought you were going to give him more salami. Fletcher foiled the flipper-footed fink!"

"Stop calling me a fink," said Nan.

"You are a real fink," said Gwen angrily. "Why did you keep wrecking our castles?"

"You never let me help you do anything," said Nan. She was angry, and she was nervous.

"It was a really mean thing to do," said Jill. "But we don't have time to argue. We have to finish our castle."

"Can I help?" asked Nan.

"No," said Gwen.

Gwen and Jill worked feverishly to finish their castle. As a final touch they made a model of Fletcher guarding the castle gates.

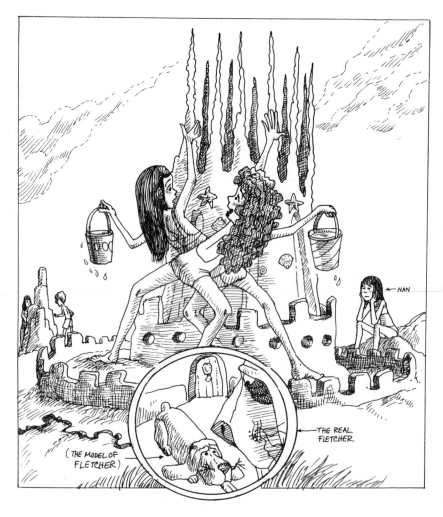

NAN

THE REAL FLETCHER

(THE MODEL OF FLETCHER)

Gwen and Jill won First Prize. George, Philip, and Joanne congratulated them. Gwen and Jill let them take turns flying their beautiful dragon kite.

As punishment for knocking down the castles, Gwen's mother wouldn't let Nan see the spectacular fireworks. Everyone else sat on the beach and watched.

Fletcher was scared of fireworks, so he hid under Nan's bed. Nan and Fletcher shared a salami all through the fireworks, and the more Fletcher ate, the less scared he was.